20 19 18 17 16 15   1 2 3 4 5 6

LIBRARY OF CONGRESS CATALOGING-IN-PUBLICATION DATA

Tireman, L. S. (Loyd Spencer), 1896–1959, author.
  Big Fat / stories by Loyd Tireman ; adapted by Evelyn Yrisarri ; layout and illustrations by Ralph Douglass.
    pages cm. — (Mesaland Series ; Book 5)
  "A facsimile of the 1947 first edition."
  Summary: "Follows the adventures of a rather large prairie dog."—Provided by publisher.
    ISBN 978-0-8263-5605-5 (cloth : alk. paper) [1. Prairie dogs—Fiction.]
  I. Yrisarri, Evelyn, adaptor. II. Douglass, Ralph, illustrator. III. Title.
  PZ7.T5167Bi 2015
  [E]—dc23
                        2015006374

WAKE UP!

Two keen eyes peered out of the tunnel. They were looking around for possible danger.

Next came a little round head.   Finally, out

popped a little prairie dog. He was known to all the town as "Little Ugly." He was small for a prairie dog, but he made up for his lack of size in other ways. This little prairie dog was a tease. He spent most of the day teasing the other prairie dogs. He particularly liked to tease his nearest neighbor, Big Fat.

Big Fat was just the opposite of Little

Ugly. He was larger than most prairie dogs, as he weighed a little over two pounds. Big Fat was very good-natured. Because he was so good-natured, he never resented Little Ugly's unkind remarks. He always had a kind word for every prairie dog in the town. Consequently, everyone liked the big prairie dog better than the little one. Perhaps that was the reason why Little Ugly treated Big Fat so badly.

It was early in the morning when Little Ugly came out of his den. He sat down on the small mound at the entrance. There was nobody in sight. As he sat looking around he snorted, "What lazy prairie dogs! Here it is almost sun-up and no one in sight!"

Little Ugly knew that Big Fat liked to sleep. "Now for some fun," thought Little Ugly. "I'll wake up one sleepy-head." He ran over to Big Fat's den. When he reached the den, he stuck his head down into the hole and whistled very loudly. Without waiting

he darted back to his own den. He sat down facing the other way. He pretended he had just come up from his den.

It wasn't long before Big Fat poked his head out. Then he came lumbering out of his den. He blinked sleepily in the morning light. He looked suspiciously across at Little Ugly. But the little prairie dog was very busy looking the other way, examining the town. Big Fat suspected that Little Ugly had played a trick on him, but he wasn't quite smart enough to figure it out.

"My, my, Little Ugly," said Big Fat, "Your whistle was so loud it woke me up. I was sure you were standing right beside me."

Little Ugly grinned wickedly to himself. He paid no attention to his friend. Slowly he

turned around inspecting the town. When he was almost face to face with Big Fat, he seemed to notice him for the first time. "Well, well, good morning, my fat friend," he said in a surprised voice, "What brings you out so early this fine morning?"

Big Fat, still suspicious, said, "Little Ugly, did you come over and whistle at me?"

Little Ugly very innocently replied, "Why should I bother a sleepy-head like you? Your

big fat stomach will let you know when it is breakfast time.'" And he disappeared into his den to prevent further questions.

"Something strange about that whistle," said Big Fat to himself. "I still think it was Little Ugly who did it. Tomorrow I'm going to get up early. If he tries it again, I'll catch him."

Little Ugly didn't need to worry about being caught. Big Fat was too lazy and too good-natured to catch him. Certainly not if it required him to get up early in the morning.

THE THORN

Big Fat, as you know, was the largest prairie dog in the prairie dog town. He was also the fattest and the laziest. He was content just to sit all day watching the rest. That is, he would have been had he not been obliged to leave his den if he expected to get anything to eat. Of

course, it was true also that he liked to hear
all the gossip. For that he could always depend
on Little Ugly. Sometimes Little Ugly even
told him where to find tender roots and grass
seeds.

One morning Little Ugly said, "Come on,
Big Fat, let's go and find something to eat."
Big Fat gave a great big sigh as he got up.

"Do we have to go far?"

"Not too far. I know where there are some
delicious prickly pears."

This made Big Fat very eager, as he dearly

loved to eat tender leaves. They hadn't gone
very far when Big Fat became tired and sat
down to rest.

"Oh! Come on," said Little Ugly, "We
have just started."

"Well, you will have to wait until I can get
my breath."

After Big Fat had rested a little, they
started on. But in a few minutes, he sat down
again.

"My goodness, now what?" asked Little
Ugly.

"Nothing," said Big Fat. "I just wanted
to rest some more." Little Ugly snorted in
disgust. He sat down also and waited.

Again they started on their way. Before

they had gone very far Big Fat sat down for the third time. "It's too hot to be wandering all over the mesa," he said.

"Well," said Little Ugly, "You certainly didn't expect to find prickly pears right next to town, did you? We still must go a little farther."

The fat prarie dog pulled himself up, grumbling, and started on. He stepped on a sharp cactus spine. "Oh! Oh!" he wailed, "How it hurts! I can't walk any more."

"Hold your foot up here," ordered Little Ugly, impatiently, "so I can pull the sticker out for you."

Gladly Big Fat held up his foot while Little Ugly removed the spine.

"Come on," said Little Ugly.

"Oh, but my foot is too sore to walk any farther."

"Think of the nice, tender, green leaves waiting for us," tempted the mean little dog. That was too much for greedy Big Fat, so on they trudged.

Soon Big Fat was ready to sit down again. By this time Little Ugly had become very impatient. As Big Fat flopped down, Little Ugly pushed a cactus stem under him. Big Fat jumped up and howled, "Oh me! I'm killed! I'm full of cactus spines." He danced up and down in real pain.

"Well, I have *never* seen you move so fast," chuckled Little Ugly.

"Oh! Do something! Quickly! Pull them out."

"Stop jumping around so I can."

He got busy and pulled out the spines. He cunningly left a few sticking in Big Fat's fur just where they could be felt most if sat upon. Of course, Big Fat didn't know they had been left.

"How much farther must we go?" asked
Big Fat.

"Just over the next hill and down the arroyo," answered Little Ugly.   Big Fat

groaned and puffed up the hill. "I can't go much farther," he said. "Think I'll sit down on this rocky ledge. I'm sure there won't be any cactus spines here."

"I wouldn't do that," said Little Ugly. "I have a feeling you might get hurt again."

"Nonsense," said Big Fat. "How could I?" But he looked the ledge over very carefully to make sure nothing would stick him. As he plumped himself down, he said, "You see, you are just trying to scare . . ." He didn't finish. Just then the spines stuck through his coat and jabbed him. "Oh me! Oh me! I'm stuck again," he howled.

"You certainly are a baby! Why there isn't a cactus anywhere near you!" scolded Little Ugly. "But turn around and I'll see what I can find."

By this time Big Fat had had enough. He had lost interest in the nice tender green stems. He started for home!

THE PUPPIES

One day Little Ugly and Big Fat met in the prairie dog town. Big Fat was beaming all over with pride.

"Why are you so happy?" asked Little Ugly.

"I'll tell you," said Big Fat. "We have the

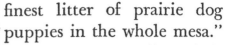

finest litter of prairie dog puppies in the whole mesa."

"Um, uh," replied Little Ugly, who hadn't any experience with puppies.

"They are the best looking, the healthiest, and the best behaved puppies on the mesa," said Big Fat. "Of course, they look and act just exactly like me," he continued modestly.

"Humph," snorted Little Ugly. "I feel sorry for them if they look and act just like you."

Big Fat was too happy to be bothered by any such remark.

"What a beautiful day this is!" "I believe I'll bring the puppies up and show them to you."

Reaching his den, Big Fat dove into his hole. Soon he appeared again. He looked around for possible enemies. Then tiny shrill barks could be heard as Big Fat said, "Come out, little ones."

As the puppies appeared, one by one, Big Fat proudly introduced them to Little Ugly:

This is Baby,
Short and fat,

This is Kitty,
Like a cat,

This is Slim,
Long and thin,

This is Blacky,
Dark as sin,

This is Peppy,
Fast as mice,

This is Tiny,
Small and nice.

Little Ugly looked them over with interest. They all looked alike to him except Blacky. "They are cute," he frankly admitted. "All roly-poly, with big bright eyes and cute tails."

Suddenly Little Ugly wished he had some puppies, too.

"Pups," said Big Fat. "This funny-looking prairie dog is your Uncle Ugly. He is a very fine prairie dog and will do anything you ask him."

Little Ugly was about to deny this when he noticed Baby Prairie Dog coming toward him. She was so cute. She was so trustful, that he loved her at once.

This was the first time the puppies had been out of the den. Even Mother Prairie Dog watched them proudly. They rolled and tumbled. They ran around in circles. In general, they behaved like other young puppies.

Little Ugly, wanting to be nice to the puppies, asked, "Would you like to go and get some green leaves to eat?"

Big Fat was shocked. He faced Little Ugly scornfully. "Why, Little Ugly, I'm surprised at you. Don't you know that these puppies are babies? They don't eat leaves yet."

"Oh," said Little Ugly very humbly. Then he brightened. "Never mind, I'll watch out

for all the nice seeds, and when you are old enough, we'll go and find them."

"Come puppies," said Mrs. Fat. "You have been out in the sunshine long enough for one day." Blacky, who was several feet away wasn't ready to go back into the den. So he sat down. His mother called again, "Come, puppies." But Blackie didn't budge. Without another word his mother went over to him, cuffed him, and sternly said, "When I call, you must come. Do you hear me?"

After they had disappeared into the hole, Big Fat remarked proudly, "Don't you think they are a wonderful family?"

"Yes, I do," said Little Ugly. "How nice that they look just like their mother."

RUN! RUN!! RUN!!!

Every day someone would remind the little prairie dogs to run.

Mother Prairie Dog warned, "Run when you hear the Watcher whistle. Run and run fast!"

Then Father Prairie Dog would add,
"Run for the den when you hear the
Prairie Dog whistle!"
The first word that Baby Prairie Dog

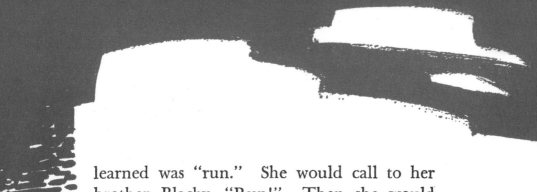

learned was "run." She would call to her brother Blacky, "Run!" Then she would scamper into the hole leading down into the den. Sometimes Blacky would follow and sometimes he wouldn't.

Late one afternoon the little prairie dogs were out playing in the sunshine. Big Fat sat on a mound watching for any sign of danger. Uncle Ugly also sat near his den watching carefully.

"It's about time for Coyote to pay us a visit," said Little Ugly.

The father prairie dog looked around anxiously. "Don't go far away," he called.

The other little prairie dogs listened. But Blacky did not listen. He was too busy. He had found a nice tender root and did not want to leave it. Besides, he was a venturesome little prairie dog. "Oh, I'm fast and can get back to the den if there is any danger," he thought. Little Blacky went on chewing the nice tender root and paid no attention to his father's warning.

Just then, from the far side of Prairie Dog Town, came a faint, but sharp, warning whistle.

Big Fat heard the warning and called, "Run!"

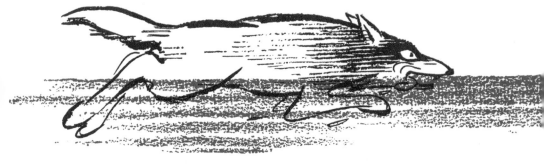

"Run!" echoed Baby Prairie Dog.

All the little prairie dogs except Blacky ran as fast as their fat little legs could carry them. They dashed into the tunnel. Blacky saw all his brothers and sisters running for home. But the whistle had been faint. He was sure it was far away. The root was delicious so he kept on chewing. He held the root in his front paws and sat up so he could watch more carefully. There was no enemy in sight. He couldn't see the slightest movement anywhere.

Of course he couldn't. Three Toes, the Coyote, was taking great care not to be seen. As he spied the fat little prairie dog, he thought, "There's a fine supper."

Three Toes was a very smart Coyote. He stopped behind a big clump of a rabbit bush. Then he detoured until he was behind the scrub cedar where Blacky was sitting. Three Toes crept up, softly, softly, softly, without a

sound until he was close to the bush. He knew the little prairie dog was on the other side, for he could hear him tearing and chewing the root. Then Three Toes dashed around the bush.

Too late, Blacky heard the scampering feet of Three Toes in the sand. He saw the huge mouth with the sharp teeth. The fat little prairie dog was terribly afraid. He tried to run, but the Coyote was too fast and grabbed him.

As soon as Blacky was missed, Big Fat came up to look for him. When he reached the entrance he saw that old Three Toes was carrying Blacky away. Slowly he turned and went back into the den.

"Blacky will not be back to play with you," he said sadly. "He didn't come when he heard the danger whistle. Now the Coyote has him."

"Didn't he run?" asked Baby Prairie Dog.

"Yes, but he waited too long," replied her father.

"And did the big bad Coyote carry him away?" inquired Baby Prairie Dog.

"Yes," said the father prairie dog. "A Coyote can run so much faster than a prairie dog that we have to start before danger is upon us or we are caught."

STUCK

It was the time of the year when it rained frequently in New Mexico. The prairie dogs didn't like this season. There was little they could do, except to stay down deep in their dens. This didn't give them very much time to gossip with their neighbors.

One day Big Fat came out and went over to Little Ugly's den. He wanted to tell him about the herd of horses seen near the village. As he was talking to Little Ugly, a few drops

of rain spattered in the sand. Big Fat started to go home. He didn't want to get his nice fur coat wet.

But Little Ugly hadn't heard enough about the horses. He begged his friend to stay. "It may not rain," said Little Ugly, "And if it does you can come down into my den. It's dry and I have some choice seeds. I'm sure you'd like them."

"That sounds like a good idea," said Big Fat and sat down to tell little Ugly some more about the wild horses.

Suddenly without warning, the clouds seemed to open and the rain poured down.

"It's raining! Run!" gasped Little Ugly.

Big Fat made a dive for the entrance to Little Ugly's den. But both prairie dogs had forgotten that the hole into Little Ugly's den was very small. Big Fat was a very large prairie dog. When he dived down through the nar-

row entrance, his head and front feet were caught in the hole.

Little Ugly was frantic. The rain was pouring down! He was sure he would drown. He tried to push Big Fat into the hole, but that only made matters worse. Poor Big Fat was frightened. There he was with his head and forefeet down the tunnel. His wet hind legs and fat stomach were all that could be seen sticking out in the rain. He just couldn't pull himself out of the hole. At every attempt, his hind legs skidded around in the mud.

Finally he made a great effort. He gave a big kick, unfortunately hitting Little

Ugly. The blow knocked the little prairie dog head over heels into the mud. This made Little Ugly furious. He jumped up and seized Big Fat's little stubby tail in his teeth. He braced himself and pulled. As he pulled, he also bit the tender tail.

Big Fat gave a squeal of pain and rage. In his excitement he backed out of the hole with a rush! Little Ugly had not expected Big Fat to come out so fast. The

mound was very slippery
and muddy. When Big Fat
backed out in such a hurry,
he fell right on top of Little
Ugly. Such a scramble!
Both prairie dogs were very
cross, very wet, and very
muddy. Forgetting all
about the rain and their dis-
comfort, they began to
quarrel.

"You pushed me and
bit me," cried Big Fat in an
angry voice.

"You jumped on me,"
hotly returned Little Ugly.

"Well," said Big Fat, "You asked me to stay when you knew your door was too small. What can you say to that?"

"You are so fat that it's a crime," said Little Ugly. "You couldn't get through an ordinary door, not to mention mine!"

Just then it stopped raining as suddenly as it had started. The bright sun came out and beamed on Prairie Dog Town. Both prairie dogs began to laugh.

"Oh, Big Fat, you really looked so funny," laughed Little Ugly, "stuck in my hole with your hind legs waving around."

"Oh, is that so?" said Big Fat. "I wish I could

have seen you when you fell into the mud!"
And they sat down and held their sides with
laughter. That was a fine way to forget a
quarrel, and they parted good friends as ever.

The End

The End